**JOSHUA JONES**

**MRS KARIA**

# MEET ALL THESE FRIENDS IN BUZZ BOOKS:

Thomas the Tank Engine
The Animals of Farthing Wood
Fireman Sam
Joshua Jones
Rupert
Babar
James Bond Junior

First published in Great Britain 1993 by Buzz Books,
an imprint of Reed Children's Books
Michelin House, 81 Fulham Road, London, SW3 6RB
and Auckland, Melbourne, Singapore and Toronto

Joshua Jones film © copyright 1990 S4C/Channel 4 Wales
Joshua Jones character © copyright 1989 Rob Lee
Text © copyright 1993 Reed International Books Limited
Illustrations © copyright 1993 Reed International Books Limited
Based on the animation series produced by Bumper Films
for S4C/Channel 4 Wales and Prism Art & Design Limited
Produced and directed by Ian Frampton and John Walker
Photographs by John Walker
All rights reserved

ISBN 1 85591 234 1

Printed in Italy by Olivotto

# SNAKE CHASE

Story by Olivia Madden
Developed from a script
by Bob Wilson

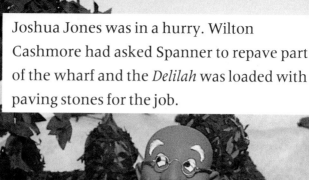

Joshua Jones was in a hurry. Wilton Cashmore had asked Spanner to repave part of the wharf and the *Delilah* was loaded with paving stones for the job.

"Coming in for a cup of tea?" asked Admirable when Josh got to the lock.

"I wish I could," said Josh, "but I've got to go straight on. The engine's been playing up and I'm a bit late already."

Regretfully, Admirable watched Josh chug off down the canal. He was admiring the departing narrow boat when he noticed a curious sheen on the water – oil! The *Delilah* was losing oil and that spelt trouble.

Admirable was on his own so there was only one way to warn Josh — go himself.

"Man the lifeboats," muttered Admirable, climbing into his rowing boat and setting off in pursuit of the *Delilah*.

Over at the veterinary clinic, Ravi was admiring a new patient, a grass snake.

"Has it got deadly poisonous fangs?"

"Of course not, Ravi," said Daphne. "Grass snakes are harmless."

There was a knock on the door.

"Hold the snake for me, Ravi," Daphne said. "That will be Joe Laski. He's going to cut the grass."

Sure enough, it was Joe, along with Fiona and Trojan. "My mower is broken," said Joe, "but Trojan can eat the grass instead, okay?"

"Let's go and watch," said Ravi to Fiona.
"Here, you can hold the snake."

"Ugh!" screamed Fiona. "Take it away."

Ravi was dancing round Fiona teasing her,
when to his horror, the snake wriggled out
of his grasp and disappeared.

"Oh no! Help me find it, Fi," he wailed.

The snake slithered under a chair and out into the garden. It slipped down the path, across the flowerbed, and onto the grass where Trojan was grazing.

For a moment, snake and horse gazed at each other in fright. Then Trojan reared up, leapt over the garden wall and cantered off down the lane.

"My Trojan! Come back!" cried Joe.

Ravi picked up the snake. "So there you
are," he said.

"Quick! Into the car, Joe. We'll go after Trojan," said Daphne.

She started the engine and held the doors open for Fiona and Joe.

"Hey! Wait for me," called Ravi as she drove down the drive and into the lane.

"You look on the towpath," shouted Daphne.

Ravi ran to his bike, deposited the snake in his bag and pedalled off as fast as he could.

15

Back at the wharf, Spanner was hard at work. He enjoyed being in charge of the cement mixer and when Sharon arrived with a thermos of tea, he didn't want to stop.

"This is a highly technical job, Sharon," he said seriously.

Just then, the mixer unexpectedly disgorged cement all over his feet. Sharon giggled.

"Oh yes, highly technical," she said.

"Spanner!" roared Wilton from his balcony.

"You should be laying those paving stones."

"I'm waiting for Josh," called Spanner.

Daphne wasn't sure which road to take.

"What do you think? Left to Grimspool?"

"Look! I think I see Trojan in that field," said Fiona, pointing.

"Okay, everybody, hang onto your hats," said Daphne as the car lurched into gear.

When Ravi reached the crossroads, he turned right down the towpath. He was most surprised to see his grandfather rowing down the canal.

"Hi, Bapu. Are you looking for Trojan?"

"No," said Admirable. "I'm looking for Josh. It's urgent!"

"I've got to warn him. The *Delilah* is losing oil and the engine will be scuppered if Josh isn't careful," said Admirable.

"Don't worry, Bapu. I'll soon catch up with him," said Ravi and he sped off down the towpath on his bicycle.

Josh looked at his watch.

"Oh dear, Fairport. If Spanner's concrete sets before we get to the wharf, I'm in big trouble. We'd better pick up speed once we're through the tunnel."

As he said this, there was a squeal of brakes and Ravi appeared on the towpath.

"Bapu says you're losing oil," he shouted.

Josh checked the oil gauge. It was falling rapidly. He was lucky Ravi had come along.

"Strewth! I'd better switch it off. Thanks, Ravi. You've saved my engine."

"So is everything all right now, Josh?" asked Ravi.

"I don't know how I'm going to deliver these paving stones on time without the engine. How will I get through the tunnel?" Josh looked glum, then his face brightened. "I know. I'll leg it."

Ravi looked bewildered. "Leg it?" he repeated, gazing at Josh.

"Jump aboard and I'll show you," said Josh. Ravi placed his bike on the boat, then hopped on board. He took the tiller and watched as Josh lay flat on his back on top of the cabin. Josh gripped the boat tightly and then started to walk, upside-down, along the roof of the tunnel. As he walked, the barge moved along beneath him.

"What a great idea!" said Ravi.

"Not mine," panted Josh. "This is how narrow boats went through tunnels before they had engines. But now we're through, how are we going to get to the wharf?"

"Look," cried Ravi, "it's Trojan!"

"Just in time. We'll make this delivery the traditional way," said Josh. "Watch this."

On the wharf, Wilton Cashmore watched as
Spanner smoothed out the concrete.
Suddenly there was a furious hooting and
Daphne's car shot round the corner.

"Out of the way, Spanner. We're in a
hurry," she shouted.

Wilton took one look and jumped to safety.

"Stop," cried Spanner helplessly. "Stop!"

Daphne slammed on the brakes, but — too late — she'd already driven over Spanner's wet cement!

Spanner gasped in surprise. "My lovely cement," he said weakly.

Suddenly, Daphne said, "Listen!"

27

Everyone was quiet. They could hear a faint clop-clop along the towpath and slowly the *Delilah* slipped into view.

"Ahoy there," said Josh. "Anyone ready for some paving stones?"

"Trojan!" said Joe Laski. "He helps Josh make the delivery. But why did he bolt?"

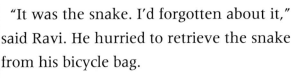

"It was the snake. I'd forgotten about it," said Ravi. He hurried to retrieve the snake from his bicycle bag.

"Do be careful, Ravi," warned Daphne. "If Trojan catches sight of that snake he'll be off, and I don't think Josh wants his barge towed all the way back to the lock!"

## SPANNER

## FAIRPORT

**FIONA CASHMORE**     **RAVI KARIA**